Computer Clues

OTHER YEARLING BOOKS YOU WILL ENJOY:

WRITE UP A STORM WITH THE POLK STREET SCHOOL,
Patricia Reilly Giff
COUNT YOUR MONEY WITH THE POLK STREET SCHOOL,
Patricia Reilly Giff
THE POSTCARD PEST, *Patricia Reilly Giff*
TURKEY TROUBLE, *Patricia Reilly Giff*
SHOW TIME AT THE POLK STREET SCHOOL,
Patricia Reilly Giff
LOOK OUT, WASHINGTON, D.C.!, *Patricia Reilly Giff*
GREEN THUMBS, EVERYONE, *Patricia Reilly Giff*
SECOND-GRADE PIG PALS, *Kirby Larson*
CODY AND QUINN, SITTING IN A TREE, *Kirby Larson*
ANNIE BANANIE MOVES TO BARRY AVENUE,
Leah Komaiko

Computer Clues

Judy Delton

Illustrated by Alan Tiegreen

A Yearling Book

Published by
Bantam Doubleday Dell Books for Young Readers
a division of
Bantam Doubleday Dell Publishing Group, Inc.
1540 Broadway
New York, New York 10036

Visit us on the Web! www.bdd.com
Educators and librarians, visit the BDD Teacher's
Resource Center at www.bdd.com/teachers

ISBN: 0-440-41339-7

Printed in the United States of America

October 1998

10 9 8 7 6 5 4 3 2 1

CWO

For Roxanne Lien:
Party giver, storyteller,
beast keeper extraordinaire!

Long live the *liens d'amitie*
among us!

Contents

CHAPTER 1

Looking for Excitement

"I wish something exciting would happen around here," said Rachel Meyers. It was autumn, and the Pee Wee Scouts were on their way to Mrs. Peters's house for their meeting. They met every Tuesday in their leader's basement. "In my cousin Courtney's school in New York, they have a computer lab," Rachel continued. "They get to do all this fun stuff using the computer."

"I know," said Patty Baker. "In Ash-

1

ley's school in California, they play computer games and send electric mail and learn about baby whales." Ashley was Patty's cousin. She was a part-time Pee Wee Scout. When she was in California, she was a Saddle Scout.

"It's not electric mail. It's electronic mail," said Kenny, Patty's twin brother. "And we can learn about whales and stuff in the encyclopedia. We don't have to have a computer."

"Pooh," said Rachel, kicking at a big pile of red maple leaves. "Books are old-fashioned. Courtney says people who still use books are roadkill on the information superhighway. She says the big cities all have state-of-the-art stuff in their schools. She says Minnesota is way behind."

"That's not true!" said Mary Beth Kelly to her best friend, Molly Duff. "People in Minnesota are just as smart as people in

New York. My mom says Minnesota is a good place for kids to grow up. There's more fresh air and lakes, and you don't get run over by taxi cabs."

"My uncle did," said Roger White. "Right on Main Street. Pow!"

None of the Pee Wees had anything to say about Roger's uncle. They were all too busy thinking about computers.

There were twelve Pee Wees. Twelve and a half counting Ashley, who came to Scout meetings only during the half year when she was visiting her cousins.

"All I know is that Minnesota is not as exciting as New York," said Rachel.

"And not as exciting as California," said Patty.

"My dad's got a computer," said Roger. "Right here in Minnesota. It has every-thing. Even Outernet."

"Outernet!" laughed Rachel. "It's Internet, not Outernet!"

Roger liked to laugh at others, but he didn't like it when others laughed at him. His face turned bright red. "Inner, Outer, what's the difference?" he said. "My dad's computer can do everything."

"Does it wash the dishes?" asked Sonny Stone. "Does it take out the garbage?"

"Hey! Does it drive a car?" roared Tim Noon.

"How about doing homework?" asked Tracy Barnes.

"It does homework," said Roger. "And it does lots of other stuff."

"My dad has a computer at the office," said Molly. "He can even use it to order groceries from the market."

"A computer can't go to the market," said Tim. "No way."

"It can," said Jody George, who was in a wheelchair. Everyone liked Jody. He was smart and he was nice. The Pee Wees liked to ride in his wheelchair. They all wished they had one, too.

"If you have a modem, you can connect with places all over the world," said Jody. "I can even put CDs in mine. I have one CD with a whole encyclopedia on it."

Molly was pleased that Jody was taking her side. She was not surprised that Jody had his very own computer. The Georges were rich. They had a big house with a swimming pool. There weren't many swimming pools in Minnesota. It was cold and snowy half the year. When Molly was old enough to have a boyfriend, she decided, it would be Jody. If she married him someday, when she was grown up, she would get to ride in his wheelchair as often as she liked.

The Pee Wees arrived at Mrs. Peter's house. They went around to the back door and down the basement steps to start their meeting. It felt good to get indoors away from the brisk fall wind.

"Hello!" called Mrs. Peters. "Hurry in. There's lots of excitement today! We are going to earn a brand new badge. Guess what it's for!"

"Tying knots?" asked Sonny.

"Hiking?" said Kevin Moe. Kevin liked the outdoors.

"Skating?" asked Tracy.

Mrs. Peters shook her head and smiled. "Something more exciting than all of those," she said. "Something brand new that we have never done. We are going to learn to use computers!"

CHAPTER 2

Meeting
Mr. Machine

The Pee Wees couldn't believe their ears! Could their leader have read their minds? Was Minnesota as up-to-date as New York and California? Would the Pee Wees be able to compete with Ashley and Courtney on the information superhighway?

"We were just talking about computers!" Kevin told Mrs. Peters. "We must have ESP!"

What in the world does *ESP* stand for?

thought Molly. *Enemy Spy Police? Enter Secret Pal? Every Sad Petunia?*

"My uncle has ESP," said Mary Beth. "When he plays cards, he always wins. He can't help it. He just knows what cards other people are holding in their hands. It's like he can see right through the cards. My dad says it's ESP. My mom says he cheats."

Many of the Pee Wees looked puzzled.

"*ESP* stands for *extrasensory perception*," said Mrs. Peters. "Mind reading. Nobody knows for sure if it's real. Sometimes it seems as if someone knows what you're thinking. But it may be just a coincidence."

Molly remembered a time last week when she had been thinking about her aunt. While she was thinking of her, there was a knock on the door. When Molly answered the door, there was her aunt!

Could that have been ESP? Could Molly herself have it? She would have to pay attention and see.

Meanwhile, the Pee Wees were excited about the computer badge.

"What do we have to do to get the badge?" asked Roger. Roger didn't like to work very hard for his badges.

"I'll tell you all about it," said their leader. "Just as soon as you take your jackets off and settle down."

"We don't have a computer, Mrs. Peters." said Tim, hanging his jacket on the back of his chair. "My mom said we can't afford one. I won't be able to get my badge if we need a computer." Tim looked as if he might cry, Molly thought.

Mrs. Peters held up her hand, a signal for quiet. "None of you need to worry about having a computer of your own. We have a computer here that we'll use." She pointed to a machine in the middle of the big desk. "And some of you have more than one computer at home that you can share with the rest of the group. If your family computer is busy, or if you don't have one, we have permission to use a computer in the high-school computer lab," she said. "The principal has set up one with our own address for electronic mail, PWS@StPaulschools.edu. *PWS* is short for *Pee Wee Scouts.* So feel free to use that computer. No one needs to buy a computer, or worry about owning one. Do you understand?"

Everyone nodded.

"Mrs. Peters, we have two computers," said Kevin. "I'm sure my dad would let someone use one of them."

"So do we," said Jody. "I'll share mine and help someone learn the software programs."

"Why is it soft?" asked Sonny. "Is it made of foam rubber, like pillows?"

The other Pee Wees looked at one another and chuckled. "Dummy," said Roger. "Software is discos you load on your computer so you can do stuff, like play games and listen to music."

"Disks," said Mrs. Peters. "But we'll go into all of that later. Right now I just want to tell you what we are going to do in the next weeks to get our new badge."

The Pee Wees sat up straight to listen. They loved new badges. And they wanted to know what they had to do to get this one. Molly didn't care how hard she had to work. It was worth it. She loved collecting bright, colorful badges. And for every badge she earned, she had learned something new.

"First of all," said Mrs. Peters, "we'll talk about some of the things that computers can do to help you. I'll also show you some basic steps so you can use computers yourselves. Then you'll have to do three things to earn your badge. The first is to write a short report, using information you find on the Internet. The second is to contact your friends via E-mail. And finally, to celebrate our new badge, we'll have a treasure hunt. All of the clues will be given to you by E-mail."

"What if we want to use a book to do research for our report?" asked Tracy.

"No books," said their leader. "Books are wonderful, but this project is all about computers. This is not a book badge. This is a computer badge. You'll find all your information on the computer, and you'll do all your writing on the computer."

Hands were waving. "Is Internet like a fishnet?" shouted Tim.

"I already know how to use a computer, Mrs. Peters," said Mary Beth.

"What kind of report?" Sonny asked.

"I'll tell you all about it," said Mrs. Peters. "And I'll introduce you to the machine."

"Hello, Mr. Machine," said Roger, putting his arm out as if to shake hands with the computer. "My name is Roger."

The Pee Wees giggled and Mrs. Peters frowned.

"Next week," she said, "we'll pick papers out of a hat. Each paper will have the subject for a report written on it. Each subject will be different. Your reports will be on items found at the fairgrounds here in town. That's where we'll have our treasure hunt. The subjects will be things like local birds or buildings or trees."

"I don't like birds, Mrs. Peters," said Tracy. "I'm allergic to feathers."

Molly could think of a million questions. How do you find something on the computer if you don't know how to spell the word? And how can you write on the computer without a pencil? How can everyone read it? Molly started to get the same scared feeling in her stomach that she got when she was in school and she didn't understand the directions for a test.

But why should she worry? Mary Beth was her best friend. And Mary Beth knew about computers!

"How do you write on a computer?" she whispered to Mary Beth.

"You need software," Mary Beth whispered back. "A program."

Programs. Software. That was no help at all. Those words didn't tell her anything!

"Mrs. Peters will explain it to us," added Mary Beth.

Of course! Mrs. Peters said she would help them! Why was Molly so impatient?

"Now let's not jump the gun," said their leader. "First things first."

Was *jump the gun* a computer term too? wondered Molly. And what did guns have to do with computers? Her mother didn't like guns. She would not be pleased if Molly had to use guns on a computer.

Most of the Pee Wees were frowning. Mrs. Peters pointed to the computer on the desk. It had a screen like a TV and a metal box. There was also something that looked like part of a typewriter. Mrs. Peters wasn't wasting any time. She pressed two buttons and the machine began to hum and lights began to flash.

"What program are you using?" asked Rachel. "We are getting a new computer that will have four different word processing programs. One of them has an entire dictionary on it. There's so much storage on the hard drive that it can hold jillions and jillions of words."

Word processing. Molly had heard about processed cheese. But how do you process words?

"Right now," said Mrs. Peters, "I just want to show everyone how to turn the computer on and off." She explained the two buttons. One for the screen. One for the hard drive.

"I can't drive, even if it's easy drive!" cried Tim. "I'm not old enough to drive!"

"*Hard drive* does not refer to driving a car," said Mrs. Peters kindly. "It means the part of the computer that stores information."

Molly was glad that there was someone who knew less than she did. Even she, Molly, knew they would not be driving a car!

CHAPTER 3

The Magic Laptop

Mrs. Peters showed the Pee Wees the little pictures on the screen. Then she held up a small plastic thing and said, "This is called a mouse."

The mouse was connected to the computer by a wire that looked like a long tail. But otherwise, it didn't look much like a mouse. For all Molly knew, *mouse* was one of those words that could be spelled two different ways. Like *moose*, the animal, and *mousse*, her mother's chocolate dessert.

"If you want to use the Internet, you take this little mouse and move it until the arrow on the screen is on this picture of a phone line," Mrs. Peters said. "Then you click the mouse twice. The Internet is full of information about all kinds of things. You will find information for your report on the Internet under www.exploreminnesota.com. Just like you would in a book about Minnesota."

Molly wanted to ask, Why not use a book, then? but she didn't.

"When you're ready to write your report, you put the arrow on this picture of a blank sheet of paper. Then you click the mouse. A blank screen will appear for you to write on. It looks just like a piece of paper." She clicked and showed them. Things whirred and buzzed. Something came on the screen, but it didn't look like a piece of paper to Molly.

Then Mrs. Peters showed them how to press buttons on the keyboard to make letters appear on the screen. It was like magic! You didn't even need a pencil. Mrs. Peters put letters together to make words. She wrote their names. Then she wrote, "The Pee Wee Scouts are all here today to learn about computers."

It was fun! Even Tim, who sometimes had trouble with his letters, could read it.

"How do you get your words onto a piece of paper?" asked Lisa Ronning.

"When you are finished writing, you turn on the printer, and put the arrow on 'print.' Then you click the mouse," said Mrs. Peters.

Mrs. Peters let everyone take a turn writing their name on the screen, along with a few sentences. Then she printed them out on real paper.

"This is easy!" said Lisa.

Molly couldn't believe it was so simple. Was it possible she had been worried for nothing?

But when it was her turn to write, Molly's mind was as blank as the screen!

Jody had written, "I like to work on computers."

Tim wrote, "Eous fun and jumpe."

Rachel wrote, "Our new computer is exciting."

When it was Molly's turn, she wrote, "I am sevenal years old."

That was wrong! She did not remember pressing the *a* and the *l*, but there they were! Now Molly's words would be printed wrong, too! They would look as silly as the words Tim had written.

"Now, boys and girls, this is a perfect time for me to show you how to correct a mistake on the screen," said Mrs. Peters.

A perfect time, the wrong Pee Wee,

thought Molly. Why hadn't Mrs. Peters corrected Tim's sentence?

Mrs. Peters pressed a button that moved the little flashing line, which was called the cursor. It went back to the word *seven*. She put the cursor on the *a* and the *l* and pressed a button labeled DELETE. The letters were gone! More magic!

"*Delete* means erase," Mrs. Peters explained. Then she printed out Molly's corrected sentence.

"And now I think that's enough work for one day. It's time for our cupcakes, our good deeds, and our song. Then we'll call it a day."

Molly put her printed message in her pocket to show her parents. It looked good, after all. No one could tell there had ever been a mistake! It was even easier and cleaner than using the pink eraser in her desk at home. She was on the way to a new computer badge! Rat's knees, she could quit worrying. At least for now.

On the way home, Mary Beth said, "I hope I get a good project when we choose our subjects next Tuesday."

"Maybe we can trade," said Molly. "I mean, if we get something we don't like."

"I don't think so," said Tracy. "Mrs. Peters doesn't like trading."

Tracy was right. Molly remembered that from other badges. Their leader didn't want the Pee Wees to trade pen pals or hobbies or even library books.

When Molly got home, she showed her paper to her mom and dad.

"Wonderful!" said Mr. Duff proudly. "Our little Molly is on the information superhighway!"

"Next week we're going to be assigned a project to get our badge," said Molly.

"We have to write a report on the computer."

"I have an idea," said her dad. "Tomorrow I'll bring home my laptop so you can practice. By next week, you'll know your way around cyberspace very well!"

Laptop? Cyberspace? Molly was confused. Her dad didn't need to bring his laptop home. His laptop was right there when he sat down. The top of his legs, where Molly sat when he read her a story, that was his laptop. And it was always right there!

When she looked puzzled, her dad explained that his computer was called a laptop because it was so small it could fit on your lap instead of on a table. It could be moved anywhere. But when he used it at home, he could connect it to a telephone line and a printer, just like a big computer.

The next afternoon the laptop computer was waiting for Molly. "All my words won't fit on that!" she said.

"Thousands of words fit on this," laughed her dad.

"Where?" asked Molly. "Where are they all?"

"They are on a teeny tiny chip inside," said her dad. "The hard drive holds just as much data as the ones in bigger models, maybe more." When Molly looked puzzled, her mother said, "Maybe you don't know what *data* means. It means the information the computer stores, or remembers. Just like you remember things."

Cyberspace was not easy to understand. But then neither was the TV. There were really no people inside that box in her living room, and yet you could see them and hear them when you turned it on.

And what about her grandma's voice on

the telephone when she called them from France? How did her voice travel all the way across the ocean on that skinny wire?

Molly sighed. She decided she couldn't figure these things out. She would just have to trust her dad. And Mrs. Peters. They were reliable, and they always told the truth. If her dad said that millions of words could live on a tiny chip (like a chocolate chip?) inside this little box, it must be so.

Molly used the little mouse control to move the arrow to the top of the screen. Then she wrote her name, pressing the letters on the keyboard. She wrote a few sentences. When she made a mistake, she pressed the DELETE button.

"This is almost the same as Mrs. Peters's computer," she said. "Except it's smaller and the letters are green."

Molly had so much fun, she couldn't stop writing things on the screen. It took her awhile to find the letters she needed. Her dad even showed her how to press a button that made all the misspelled words jump up and scramble themselves into the right order! Cyberspace was definitely magic! This should really be good for Tim, who had so much trouble spelling.

That night Molly stayed up late in front of the laptop. She usually wrote what she had done that day, and what she thought about, and any problems or worries she had (she always had some of those), in the little diary in her desk.

"Maybe I could have a diary on the computer," she said to her mom.

"Of course," said her mom. "It's called a journal."

"But if I turn off the computer, will it all

go away and not come back?" asked Molly.

Her mom shook her head. "You press this SAVE button," she said, showing her where it was. "Now what you wrote will come back when you turn on the machine. All you have to do is press the name of the file. We'll call this file 'Molly's Journal.' "

Cyberspace was getting more exciting by the moment. At last her dad said, "That's enough for one day." Molly got ready for bed. All night she dreamed about hard drives and superhighways and Internets and disks and files. In the morning she rushed down to see if her journal was still there. Sure enough, when she turned on the machine, put the arrow on "Molly's Journal," and clicked the mouse, the whole thing popped up on the screen!

But what would the subject of her report be? What if it was something she didn't like at all, like Minnesota snakes? And would the Internet be as easy to use as her journal had been?

Next Tuesday she'd find out!

CHAPTER 4

Too Many Birds!

All week the Pee Wees practiced using their computers. Some worked on their computers at home. Some worked on Mrs. Peters's computer. And some used Kevin's and Jody's. By Tuesday they were all eager to start their reports.

When they got to the meeting, one of Mr. Peters's baseball caps was lying on the table. The hat was filled with little white slips of paper. They were folded in half so no one could see what was written on them.

"I want to read what's on those, and then choose the one I like the best!" shouted Sonny.

But Mrs. Peters held the hat high over her head. "No sirree bob!" she said.

"My name isn't Bob!" cried Sonny.

"That's just an expression," said Rachel, rolling her eyes.

"I think choosing the topics for our reports should be the first order of business," said their leader. "Then we'll learn how to find information on the Internet. Line up," she said, "and each of you draw one slip of paper."

The Pee Wees let Jody go first. When he unfolded his paper, he said, "Oh, great!"

"Jody would say 'great' no matter what topic he picked," said Mary Beth. "He never complains about stuff."

"My report is going to be about carousels. And I love them!"

"Who wants to find out about selling carrots?" grumbled Tim.

The Pee Wees stared at Tim. Sometimes it took awhile to figure out how his mind worked. Sometimes he was very deep.

Mrs. Peters smiled. "Not carrots, Tim. Carousels are merry-go-rounds. All of your reports will be on things we can find at our fairgrounds here in St. Paul."

One by one the Pee Wees drew the slips of paper.

Rachel's subject was jugglers. She frowned. "There's no juggler at the fairgrounds," she said.

"Not right now," said their leader. "But when the carnival comes to town, there are always jugglers."

"I should have picked that," said Tracy. "I can juggle four oranges at once."

Tim drew a slip that had the word

clowns. Sonny's subject was Minnesota reptiles. "I love snakes!" he said.

"All the good stuff will be gone before we get to draw," grumbled Roger.

"That's dumb," said Kenny. "No one knows what's written on the papers. How could they choose the best ones?"

"They will," said Roger stubbornly.

"Roger always makes everything into trouble," said Tracy. "My mom says some people are like that. They gripe about everything, even if it's good."

Molly closed her eyes and reached into the hat. She crossed the fingers on her left hand for luck. She wanted a good subject to write about.

"Hurry up," said Roger, giving Molly a push. Molly didn't want to hurry.

"What's the difference what subject you choose, anyway?" whispered Mary Beth.

"It's easy to find information about anything on the Internet."

That might be true. But some things would be more fun than others, thought Molly. Finally she took a paper. She didn't open it, though. She put it into her pocket. She decided to wait until she got home to read what was on it.

Mary Beth drew a slip that said *Ferris wheels*. Molly was very, very glad she hadn't drawn that! She didn't like machines. Especially machines that went high in the air. But Mary Beth seemed happy.

Roger's subject was cotton candy. Patty drew dairy products. "Ice cream!" she said.

"Does everyone have a slip of paper?" asked Mrs. Peters. She looked around. Everyone did. Roger picked up the empty hat and put it on his head.

"Now I'll show you how to do your report," Mrs. Peters said.

"I already know how," said Rachel.

"Jody knows too, but he isn't bragging about it," whispered Mary Beth to Molly.

"That's the way Rachel is," said Molly.

Mrs. Peters turned on the machine. Using the mouse, she clicked on the word "start." Then she clicked on the symbol for "Internet." Some bright, colorful words flashed onto the screen. "I am your search engine," it said. "Tell me what you want to learn."

"Now, do you see this box?" asked their leader. "You place the little flashing arrow in the box. Then you type in the subject you want information on. Suppose I want to find out about Minnesota birds. I type the word "birds" in the box." Mrs. Peters typed it in.

"Now I will put the flashing arrow on

'search' and click it once with the mouse."
She did. Click went the mouse. And very
quickly, a long list of words rolled out on
the screen. They all had to do with birds.

"I can't read all those words," said
Patty. "Some of them are too long."

"If the words are too hard," said Mrs.
Peters, "you can skip them and go on to
words you know. The Internet has more
information than you need. You should
use only what you can understand. And
you can also ask your parents, or me, to
help you with difficult words."

The Pee Wees looked at all the information about birds. "These are categories,"
said Mrs. Peters.

"The insides of cats?" asked Tim. "The
gory stuff like blood?"

The Pee Wees began to say "Yuck" and
"Ick." Their leader explained, "A *category*
is a division. Like the different places

birds live. In a nest, or a birdhouse, or a barn loft. Then there is the food birds eat, and the names of the different birds themselves. You have to decide what you want to know. You put the cursor on that line and click the mouse. Let's try 'kind of bird.' "

Mrs. Peters put the arrow on "kind" and clicked. A new list appeared. Up and down the screen were names of birds in alphabetical order. All kinds of birds, from orioles to wrens to grackles. Names of birds flew by.

"There are way too many birds!" cried Sonny.

"That's all right," said Mrs. Peters. "You simply click on the kind of bird you want to write about, and a picture of that bird will appear. And there'll also be a lot of information about the bird—what it eats and where it lives and what kind of song it sings. So in your report, you could write, 'The robin has an orange breast. It lives in Minnesota in the summer and flies south for the winter. Robins eat worms.' "

"Can't we write more than that, Mrs. Peters?" asked Rachel, frowning. "I think a report should have more information than that."

"You can make your report as long or as short as you like," said their leader. "And if you can't find the information you want, you can click on 'dictionary' or 'encyclopedia.' You will find even more information there."

"I can't wait to type in 'snakes'!" said Sonny.

Molly felt the paper in her pocket. She hoped the computer would have piles of stuff about—well, whatever it was that was on her little slip of paper!

CHAPTER 5

Lost in Cyberspace

When she got home, Molly went up to her room and shut the door. Then she took the little paper from her pocket and opened it. There was just one word written on it. Was it French? How did Mrs. Peters expect her to read French? Molly began to panic.

Then Molly noticed she was holding the paper upside down. It was just like Molly to think the worst right away! Her mother and teachers always shook their heads and said, "That wild imagination is going to get Molly in trouble someday." But sometimes her imagination was a good thing. Like when she wrote a story or drew a picture. Then everyone said, "What a wonderful imagination!"

When the paper was right side up, she could read what it said. *Barns*. What in the world could she say about barns, except that they were big and red and filled with animals and hay and smelled bad? This was not the exciting subject she had wanted.

Molly sighed. Roger may have been right. The other kids got the best subjects for their reports. *Barns* wasn't as bad as *snakes*, but it was close.

The laptop was on Molly's desk. She turned it on. She tried to remember what her dad and Mrs. Peters had said to do next. She moved the arrow along the little

row of pictures at the top of the screen. Where was the Internet picture? A lot of the pictures looked alike. Molly's nose began to itch because she was nervous. She reached up to scratch it. As she did, her hand that was holding the mouse jerked, and she clicked the button by mistake.

All of a sudden the screen filled up with lots of pictures and charts and graphs. Then they went away and lots and lots of words appeared. They were big words. Words like *data* and *license* and *finance* and *real estate* and *taxes*. None of these words had barns in them. Molly wanted all of these strange words on the screen to disappear. How could she get rid of them? She pushed buttons on the keyboard. Then she clicked the mouse. More things popped up on the screen, but nothing went away. And there was no sign of barns or Minnesota or fairgrounds. Or even the Internet! Molly was definitely in some strange land in cyberspace. A land where she was not at home. And she wanted to get out.

Suddenly she remembered Mrs. Peters showing them the DELETE button. *Delete* meant erase. Molly pressed the button. Only one letter disappeared—the letter the little flashing line was on. When she moved the arrow to another letter with the mouse, she could erase that too. But it would take her a zillion years to erase every letter, one by one.

Molly sighed and decided to begin. Slowly the letters began to disappear. But then she hit another button and the letters she had just erased all came back! She felt like crying. How in the world could she get rid of all these awful words?

She decided she would just have to try pressing more buttons and clicking on more pictures. *Tap tap. Click click.* Pictures flashed on the screen. Sometimes a question appeared, like "Do you want to delete this document?" Well, if *delete* meant erase, and *document* meant all these words, the correct answer to this question was yes, of course! She pressed "yes." The screen was clear. The words were gone. She would never have to see them again!

But what if they had been important words? Her dad's words? If her dad had saved the words, as Molly did with her journal, everything should be all right. But where had the words gone?

Molly frowned. She would have to think about that later. There was no use asking for trouble ahead of time. Maybe her dad would never miss those words. He had a lot of other words. He might not even notice. Meanwhile, she had a report to write. A report on barns. Barns in St. Paul. Barns at the fairgrounds.

This time Molly looked at all the little pictures on the screen before she clicked the mouse. She found the Internet picture and clicked on it. When the box showed up on the screen, she carefully typed the word "Minnesota" in it. Then she put the little flashing arrow on "search" and clicked the mouse. The machine whirred and whizzed and hummed and clicked and flashed red letters that said, "Searching." After a while words came onto the screen. But not as many as with "birds." She clicked the mouse on "local landmarks." There were statues and courthouses and old houses. There were pictures of the Mississippi River and the Ford plant. But no barns. Definitely no barns. What was Mrs. Peters thinking, asking a poor little Pee Wee to find something like a barn on the computer? The machine was filled with millions of birds and rivers and who knew what else?

Molly decided to click on the word "encyclopedia" instead. The cover of an encyclopedia showed up on the screen. It had a big picture of a globe on its cover. Underneath the picture was the word "subject," with a box beside it. Instead of turning actual pages, thought Molly, she was supposed to type in what she wanted to read about. Molly typed in "barns." And there in front of her was a picture of a big red barn! But it was a barn in Idaho!

Molly moved the arrow to "next page" and then clicked the mouse. That was even worse. It showed the plans for building a barn. Molly didn't want to build a barn. At least Mrs. Peters hadn't asked the Pee Wees to do anything that hard.

There were lots of pages about barns,

but nothing about barns near the fair-grounds. She would have to ask her dad for help.

Just at that moment, she heard steps on the stairs. There was a knock at her door. It was her dad.

I think I do have ESP, said Molly to herself. I wanted my dad to help me, and here he is, just like that! There was definitely something to this ESP thing.

"Hi," said her dad. "I didn't want to bother you, but it's dinnertime. Time to wash up."

"I was just thinking about you coming up here, and you did!" said Molly.

"Well, there are only two other people here besides you, so chances were pretty good it would be me," said her dad, smiling.

Molly shook her head. "It's ESP," she said. "Like mind reading."

Her dad looked skeptical. "I don't think so," he said. "It's not ESP. It's dinner!"

"I need help with my report," said Molly.

"After we eat," said Mr. Duff. "Right now you need a break and some food."

As Molly washed her hands, she thought, ESP is easy! If it was this easy, she could be in magic shows. She could read her teacher's mind and get A's on all her tests.

"I knew you were coming," said Molly to her dad when they got to the table.

Mr. Duff ruffled Molly's hair. "That's because you have an alarm clock in your stomach and you were hungry," he laughed.

But Molly wasn't that hungry. She was psychic—she knew what other people were thinking or doing before they told her. She knew that for sure.

"For supper I made one of my—" But Molly stopped her dad in mid-sentence. She closed her eyes and concentrated. "You made homemade pizza!" she cried.

Her dad nodded. "I'll bet you smelled it," he said.

Molly shook her head. "I have ESP," she said mysteriously. "I didn't smell it or see it."

Molly was learning a lot more in Pee Wee Scouts than how to use a computer. She was learning to read minds.

"I think you smelled it baking," said Mr. Duff.

"I did not!" said Molly.

Molly and her mom and dad ate almost all the big pepperoni pizza. Molly found she was hungrier than she had thought. Using the computer, and thinking so hard, took a lot of energy.

CHAPTER 6

ESP to the Rescue!

At dinner Molly told her parents about her topic. "Barns," she said.

"I love old barns," said Mrs. Duff. "They remind me of staying at my grandparents's farm in Norwood. Sometimes we'd sleep overnight in the hayloft."

"I need to find out about barns around here," said Molly. "And all I can find are barns in Idaho."

"I can help with that," said her dad. "Right after the dishes."

"Good," said Molly.

When they finished eating, Molly said to her mom, "I'll bet you're going to ask me to clear the table."

"Why yes!" she said. "I was going to ask you to do that so we can have some ice cream."

"With chocolate sauce," Molly continued.

"Yes," said her mother. "You're way ahead of me tonight!"

"Molly is psychic," said her dad. "She has ESP."

"Did you learn about that in school?" asked Mrs. Duff.

"In Scouts," said Molly. "We knew what our new badge would be even before Mrs. Peters told us."

Molly cleared the table and got the ice cream from the freezer. She was eager to get back upstairs to finish her report. She ate her dessert quickly. Then her mom said, "Why don't I do the dishes while you two work on your report?"

Molly and her dad went up to Molly's room.

"Now, I think we have to look under 'Minnesota.' Then 'barns,'" said Mr. Duff. He was almost right. They had to try several words before they found any information they could use.

"You can't give up when you're looking for something," said Mr. Duff. "If it isn't under one thing, you have to try another. It takes awhile sometimes."

But sure enough, historical barns turned up under "Minnesota's historical buildings." There was one very old cattle barn at the fairgrounds that had been built in 1900 and was still in use. It was made of concrete, and it was gray, not red.

Molly also found a building at the fairgrounds that used to be a barn, back when there was a private farm on the land. Now it was used as a pavilion and snack bar during carnivals and fairs and some ball games in the summer. It didn't look much like a barn anymore, but Molly knew that's what it used to be.

Molly thanked her dad for helping her. She decided to write her report, now that she had found the right place on the Internet.

Molly took a lot of notes and wrote down lots of barn facts. She learned that there was a poultry barn and a horse barn and a sheep barn. There was even a barn that used to house the animals and their owners when people brought their prize pets to the fair from out of town. Then she opened a blank page on the computer. She began her report by writing down the most important information.

When she finished writing, she had several pages. She pressed the SAVE key and the PRINT key. There was her report, all ready to be turned in on Tuesday. She stretched her arms and yawned. Then she turned off the laptop.

There was a rap on her door.

"Molly, I have to use the laptop for a little while tonight to check the stock market," said her mom.

"Okay," Molly said. "My report is finished."

"You work fast!" said her mom. She picked up the laptop and carried it downstairs. Molly took a warm bath and crawled into bed, with thoughts of barns and ESP all jumbled together in her head. Just as she was nodding off for the night, her mom stuck her head in the door to say good night.

"By the way," Mrs. Duff said. "One of

our documents is missing from the computer. Dad and I can't seem to find it. I don't imagine you know anything about that, do you?" When Molly didn't answer, her mother headed back downstairs.

Molly had completely forgotten about all those words that had disappeared from the screen. She was wide awake now. How in the world could she get those words back onto the laptop? Should she march downstairs and confess what had happened? Should she admit she had been careless? Or should she try to put the whole thing out of her mind and go to sleep? But how could she sleep when she was so worried?

What if those words were very important, and they were gone forever? Would her family lose money on the stock market? Would the tax people come and arrest them and put them all in jail? Where in the world did those words go? Molly couldn't think of any place she could start looking. They could be in the basement or in the attic, or even floating in the air over the house. They could be hiding in some cloud over the ocean. Even *in* the ocean itself.

If Molly really had ESP, she would be able to concentrate and get the words back, no matter where they had gone. It was worth a try. Molly buried her head in her pillow and closed her eyes very tight. She could see some of the words in her mind's eye, marching along the screen. She thought and thought about them but nothing happened. Tears came to Molly's eyes. Her parents would never trust her with the computer again. She would have to go back to using books and a pencil and paper and snail mail—the old-fashioned way of writing to people.

Molly pictured all the Pee Wees reading and writing in cyberspace, while she was sharpening a yellow pencil in Mrs. Peters's basement.

She decided to give her search one more try. "Come back, come back, come back!" she yelled. It seemed as if it must be midnight, but Molly's little alarm clock showed it was only nine. When she was just about to give up on her ESP, her dad called to her.

"Molly, are you asleep? Can you come down here a minute?"

They must know what she had done. Maybe it was her *dad* who had ESP, not Molly. Maybe he knew she had erased those words.

Molly went downstairs.

"Molly, one of our files is missing, and we can't seem to get it back. We have it saved on a backup disk, so it's not really lost. But I thought we should talk about being careful not to press the DELETE key in the wrong place when you are using the computer."

Then they did know! They did have ESP! But if the words were on this little disk, why were they so worried?

"I did it!" cried Molly. "I wanted to get all those words off the screen and I pushed the DELETE button by mistake."

Her dad frowned. "I'll show you what to do when that happens," he said. He turned the laptop on and showed Molly how to press the ESCAPE button and clear the screen without losing any important words.

"It wasn't your fault," said Mrs. Duff. "You can't learn everything about computers in a few hours."

Molly sighed. "I guess not," she said.

"We just wanted you to know that we

have the words saved on this disk," Mr. Duff said. "We know what a worrier you are, and we were afraid you wouldn't be able to sleep if you thought you had done something wrong."

"I'll be really careful next time," said Molly, giving her parents a hug and going back to bed.

As she crawled into bed, she remembered something. Just at the moment she was concentrating the hardest on those lost words, her dad had called her downstairs to tell her about the disk that the words were on. Her concentration had paid off. She did have ESP after all!

The next morning on the way to school, Mary Beth asked Molly what her report was on.

"Barns," said Molly. "And I'm all done with my report."

Mary Beth didn't seem interested in

barns. And she didn't have any questions to ask Molly about them. She probably thinks they're boring, thought Molly.

"Ferris wheels were fun to look up," said Mary Beth. "Lots of people get sick on them. Especially when they stop at the top."

Once they got to school, the girls forgot about computers. School didn't mix with Pee Wee Scouts. And it wasn't half as much fun.

CHAPTER 7

Snail Mail Out— E-mail In

After school the Pee Wees talked about their computer reports again. Some of the Scouts had not started their projects yet, but some of them were finished.

"There's piles of stuff about jugglers," said Rachel. "I could even order tickets on the computer to see a juggler next year at the fair!"

"Molly's report is about barns," said Mary Beth. No one said anything. "And mine is about Ferris wheels."

Everyone wanted to hear about Ferris wheels. Molly didn't need ESP to tell she had a boring subject for her report. Even Ferris wheels were more exciting than barns.

Roger was pretending to be a fortune-teller. "You will be a race car driver and lose all the races," he said to Sonny.

"I will not!" shouted Sonny. "I'll win them all!"

"Will not," said Roger.

"Will too," said Sonny. "You don't know how to tell fortunes. Fortune cookies are better. I had one that said I was going to be really rich."

"Hey, I have more talent than a fortune cookie!" said Roger. "I had a teacher in my other school who was a mind reader. She called me a troublemaker and she didn't even know me yet!"

"She probably had ESP," said Molly to

Mary Beth. "If she could tell that Roger was a troublemaker."

The Pee Wees changed the subject and began to talk about their own reports. Rat's knees! Who wanted to listen to stuff about snakes and dairy farming? But even those things sounded more fun than barns. At least Molly would get a badge. That was what counted.

At the next Pee Wee meeting, Mrs. Peters collected the reports that were finished. "Molly, you got my favorite subject—old barns! Did you have a good time doing it?"

Molly nodded. She didn't tell Mrs. Peters about erasing Dad's file. And she didn't tell her how ESP had helped solve the problem. Molly thought it was best to keep some things to herself—at least for now.

"Well, we are on the way to our computer badge!" said their leader with a smile. "When we are finished, you will all be computer experts!" Tim was frowning. "Well, at least you'll be on speaking terms with the machine," she added.

"Now, today we are going to learn all about E-mail. It is just like writing a real letter and mailing it, but it's much faster. The *E* stands for *electronic.* We mail these letters electronically. If we write a letter on paper, we have to find an envelope and write the address on it. Then we have to seal it and buy a stamp and go to the mailbox and mail it. And we often have to wait several days until it gets to where it's going. Sometimes it even goes to the wrong address."

"That can't happen with E-mail," said Rachel. "When my dad was in Israel, I wrote him an E-mail, and he got it just like this." Rachel snapped her fingers. "If I had mailed it snail mail, it would have taken over a week to get there. He would have been back home before it even reached him!"

The Pee Wees were impressed.

"How could a letter get there just like that?" said Sonny, snapping his fingers the way Rachel had.

Mrs. Peters smiled and turned on the computer. She clicked the mouse on the "Internet" symbol. When a row of small pictures came on, she clicked on a symbol that said "E-mail."

"This is all you do," she said, showing the Pee Wees how to use the mouse to place the arrow correctly. "Now we will click on 'new message.'" She did. Something that looked like a piece of stationery appeared on the screen. There was also a little picture of an address book.

"I'll put the little arrow on 'address book' now and click once," she said.

The Pee Wees watched. A list of names came on the screen. They looked just like the names in Molly's address book at home.

"Now, you choose who you want to write to and click on that name. It will pop to the top of the sheet and the machine will send your letter to that address automatically."

She clicked on the name "Mrs. Duff." Molly's mother's name appeared in the address box.

"All I do is write a regular letter. Dear Mrs. Duff," she wrote. "We are at our Scout meeting and we are learning E-mail. We decided to write to you at your office. Are you working hard? Have a nice day. Love from the Pee Wees."

"Now," said Mrs. Peters, "our letter is finished. What do we need to do next?"

Hands waved. "We have to print it out, like our reports," said Tracy.

"No, we don't have to print it out," said their leader. "Then it would be a regular letter needing a stamp. What we do is mail this, right from the machine!"

"Wow!" said the Pee Wees.

"It's like magic!" said Kenny.

"We just put the little arrow on this picture of an envelope with wings," she said, "and click once. Then we click on the word 'send.' "

As the Pee Wees watched, she did this. A little picture of an envelope with wings sailed across the screen from one side to the other. They read words that said, "Sending message."

"And now," said Mrs. Peters, "Mrs. Duff is reading her letter."

"Naw," said Roger. "No way."

But in a few minutes, as the Pee Wees

76

watched, a note appeared on the screen. It said, "Receiving one message." And then, just like magic, there was a new letter. It was a letter from Molly's mother.

"Dear Pee Wees," it said. "I just got your letter. I am glad you are learning how to use E-mail. I am working hard, but I wish I was outside. It is a fine, sunny day. Have a good time. Love, Mrs. Duff. P.S. Molly, don't forget to clean your room when you get home!"

The Pee Wees giggled. Molly's face turned red.

"Was that ever fast!" said Patty.

"An E-mail letter can go anywhere in the world in just a few minutes," said Mrs. Peters. "It doesn't even cost as much as a stamp."

"I want to write to my uncle!" said Roger.

"I do too," said Tim.

"You have to be sure they have a computer that's hooked up to the Internet," said Jody.

"That's right," said Mrs. Peters. "That's the only catch. You have to write to someone who has a computer. But every day more and more people are getting hooked up to the Internet." She showed them how easy it was to answer a letter using E-mail.

Then she let each of the Pee Wees write an E-mail letter to Mr. Peters at his office. After they finished, and Mr. Peters had written back, they had cupcakes and sang their Pee Wee song. Before they left for the day, their leader said, "This week I want each of you to write and send an E-mail letter all by yourself."

"Who should we send it to?" asked Jody.

"You can write to whoever you like. I want you to press the PRINT button afterward so you can bring a copy of your letter to our meeting next Tuesday."

"Do we bring a copy if we get a letter back from someone?" asked Lisa.

"Yes, I think that would be a good thing. It would help us understand how easy and fast it is to communicate," she said. "And it's fun."

"Mrs. Peters, I could just print out some of the E-mails I've sent before and bring them. I send E-mail all the time," said Rachel.

Mrs. Peters frowned. She didn't like shortcuts. "I want you to write and send a new one, Rachel. With the current date on it."

Rachel nodded.

The Pee Wees' heads were swimming with E-mail talk. Molly was thinking about who she would write to.

"Do we get extra credit if we send more than one letter?" asked Rachel.

"Send one, or however many you want, but you don't get extra credit. This isn't school. You just get your badge," their leader answered.

No extras was fine with Molly. One badge would be all she'd need. She only hoped she wouldn't erase any of her parents' E-mails while she was using the laptop!

CHAPTER 8

Molly's Secret Admirer

On the way home, all the Pee Wees could talk about was who to write to.

"Maybe I'll write to my dad's friend in Africa," said Roger.

"Hey, no E-mail goes that far!" said Sonny. "Not to the jungle with all those trees and wild animals. Some animal would jump up and eat it!"

"Animals don't eat E-mail," scoffed Kevin.

"I might write to my dad at work," said Mary Beth. "But that isn't very exciting."

"We don't get extra credit for being exciting," said Tracy. "We get our badge if we write to Africa or to the woman next door."

Molly thought she might write to Jody. Kevin would be her second choice. True, her mother had said she was too young to have boyfriends. But when someone was as nice as Jody and Kevin, it was good to plan ahead. People should marry someone they've known a long time. When her aunt got divorced last year, her dad said it was because she had hardly known the man when she married him. Molly didn't want to make that mistake. No sirree bob. She would plan ahead. She would send her letter to Jody.

At the corner, the Pee Wees separated

and went to their own houses. Molly remembered her mother's E-mail about cleaning her room. She did that first. Then she sat down and turned on the laptop. Molly liked the cozy hum it made while it was warming up. A computer wasn't a book, but Molly was liking it better every day.

Molly clicked on NEW MESSAGE. Then she clicked on Jody's name in the address book. Her dad had put the addresses of all the Pee Wees who had E-mail into the file for her.

Molly wondered what to write. She didn't want to say something mushy like, "I like you a lot because you're so nice." Or something practical like, "I want to ride in your wheelchair more often." She had to think a long time. Then she wrote a letter. But when she read it, she pressed DELETE. It wasn't what she wanted to say.

The screen was blank again. "Dear Jody," she wrote for the second time. "How are you? I am fine."

That felt pretty boring, but it was better than being too friendly. She didn't want Jody to think she had a crush on him— even if she did. It was best to stick to safe subjects. "I just cleaned my room. Have to go now and set the table for supper. Sincerely, your friend, Molly Duff."

Setting the table wasn't very interesting. Jody would think all she did in her free time was housework. She changed that line to "I have to go and eat supper." But that was a lie. Her mom wasn't even home yet. Molly sighed. It wasn't that long until supper. She'd send the message the way it was. Molly pressed SPELL CHECK, and any misspelled words jumped into place. Boy, pretty soon kids won't have to go to school at all, she thought. Who needs to learn how to spell if the computer does it for you? And who needs math when a little calculator adds and subtracts and multiplies and divides?

Molly clicked on the word "send." Jody's message flew across the screen and out into space, and from there it hopped right into his computer. Molly hoped Jody's dad wasn't using the computer. Oh well, she hadn't said anything personal.

After the machine sent the message, some words appeared that said, "Message sent" and "Checking mail." Sure enough, Molly had mail! A letter came onto the screen. The return address was PWS@StPaulschools.edu. Why would she be getting mail from a school? Maybe it was for her dad. But it didn't look that way. It said "Dear Molly" at the top.

Then Molly remembered. The Pee Wee Scouts had a special computer set up in the high-school computer lab. The *PWS* stood for *Pee Wee Scouts.* Mrs. Peters had told them they could use it anytime. Some Pee Wee Scout was using that computer now.

"Dear Molly," the message said. "I liked the shirt you had on today. It was really cool. Plaid is my favorite color. You have lots of cool stuff. I have a new pet. It's a turtle. Its name is Ralph. Do you have a turtle? Well, I have to go now. Love from a secret admirer."

Who was this? It had to be one of the Pee Wees. But which one? Molly wondered if it was Jody. It didn't sound like Jody. Unless it was a disguise. Jody had more pets besides turtles. And she was sure his favorite color wasn't plaid. Maybe he was joking. How would she find out?

As she sat there puzzled, another message popped onto the screen. This one *was*

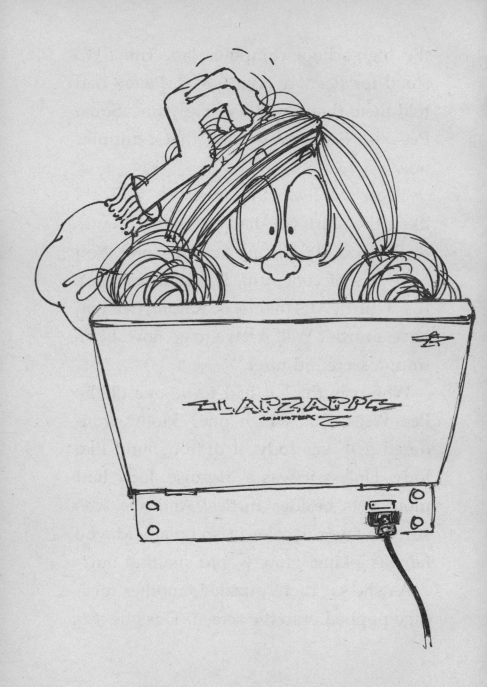

from Jody. The real Jody! "Dear Molly," it said. "I just got your letter. Thanks for writing to me. Scouts was fun today. But then it always is. It's a lot of fun to earn new badges. Well, write back when you get time. Sincerely, Jody."

Jody had answered her. He wanted her to write back to him. Rat's knees, E-mail was fun! But Jody's writing did not sound anything like the secret admirer's writing. The admirer must be someone different.

Now Molly had sent a letter, and she had gotten a letter back. She printed both of them out, to take to the next Pee Wee meeting.

But what about that other letter? Should she answer it? Should she take a copy of that one to Scouts too?

And who in the world could her secret admirer be? If Molly's ESP was worth anything, she should be able to figure out who this admirer was. She closed her eyes and thought and thought. But no name came to her through the air waves.

She called Mary Beth and asked her if she had sent her a joke E-mail.

"Of course not!" said her best friend. "I might send one to Roger, but not to you."

"Maybe Roger sent it," said Molly. "But he'd never admit it."

Molly didn't feel like writing or calling Roger. If it was him, or even if it wasn't, he would just tease her and tell everyone that she liked him.

"It could be Tim," said Mary Beth. "I think his favorite color is plaid."

"But he's not a joker," said Molly. "And the message was written in real sentences."

"How about Sonny?" her friend asked.

"It could be him. Or Kevin. Or Kenny," admitted Molly.

"Well, I know it isn't Rachel," said Mary Beth. "She never fools around like that."

The girls hung up the phone.

All week Molly tried to find out who her secret admirer was. All week she practiced ESP to see if it would help. But Tuesday came and still she had not been able to come up with anything.

At Pee Wee scouts, Mrs. Peters looked at all the E-mails. Almost everyone had one. Some of the Pee Wees had two or three. Everyone but Rachel.

"Rachel?" said Mrs. Peters. "Do you have yours? I thought you would be the first one to bring in an E-mail and a reply."

Hearing this, Rachel flung a piece of paper onto the table and burst into tears.

CHAPTER 9

"Oops!"

The Pee Wees were used to seeing Rachel in control of things. This was the first time they had seen her so upset.

"Maybe her mom is in the hospital," Tracy whispered to Molly.

"Maybe her parents are getting divorced," said Lisa.

"Her dad's a dentist," Kenny scoffed. "Dentists don't get divorced."

"Dentists can get divorced just like anybody else," said Patty. "Who says they don't?"

The paper lay on the table. No one touched it. Maybe Rachel was in trouble with the police, thought Molly. Maybe she had been caught shoplifting. No, that was silly. Rachel had all the clothes she wanted. But then Molly remembered hearing on TV once that most shoplifters don't need the stuff they steal. They take things to get attention.

"Just read this!" cried Rachel. "He said I was stuck-up! He said my legs were fat! They aren't! I have a dancer's legs!"

Rachel put her head down on the table and wept. Mrs. Peters went over and put her arms around her.

"Of course you do," Mrs. Peters said. She picked up the paper and read it. "This E-mail went to the wrong person. I forgot to warn you that mistakes can be made using E-mail. The writer meant to click on Roger's name in the address book, but instead he pressed Rachel's. So Roger never got the message. Rachel got it instead."

"And it's all a bunch of lies!"

"Of course it is," said Mrs. Peters. "And what's more, those things are rude and impolite and should not be said to anyone. Especially in Pee Wee Scouts, where we are good to others."

"There are worse things than having fat legs," said Lisa. "It would be worse if Rachel had two heads or something."

Rachel stamped her foot under the table. "But I *don't* have fat legs!" she cried.

A hum was going through the room. Everyone was saying the same thing: "Who wrote that nasty letter to Roger?"

Wasn't the sender's name at the top of the letter? It should be. Unless, like the message from Molly's secret admirer, it had been sent from the high school.

Soon everyone knew who had sent the letter, because all of a sudden Sonny turned bright red and ran from the room.

Mrs. Peters turned on the computer. She showed them how easy it was to make the mistake of clicking the mouse while the arrow was on a name above or below the name you wanted. "You have to take your time and double-check what you say and who your letter is going to. You have to be sure you are really ready to press SEND before you do. But even more important, it is never wise to say mean things about others."

Rachel wiped her eyes and combed her hair. Mrs. Peters didn't talk about the bad letter any longer. They went on to other things, then told about their good deeds and sang the Pee Wee song. They were just about ready for their treats when Mrs.

Stone came down the steps, dragging Sonny by his ear. Now Sonny was the one who was crying.

"Sonny has something to say to Rachel, and to all of the Pee Wees," she said. Sonny looked as if he didn't have anything to say. His mother gave him a nudge.

"I'm sorry!" he said. His mother nudged him again. "I wrote it to Roger, not Rachel."

Now Mrs. Stone nudged him harder. "I don't know why I said that stuff. Rachel doesn't have fat legs." Sonny sat down and put his head in his hands. Mrs. Stone went upstairs to get the cupcakes.

"He didn't say she wasn't stuck-up, though," whispered Mary Beth to Molly. Her friend was right. But then, Rachel *was* stuck-up. Even though Sonny should not

have said so, it was true. It would be hard to take that back.

Mrs. Peters clapped her hands. "Watch your E-mail this week," she said, "for clues about our treasure hunt. The treasure is hidden somewhere in the fairgrounds. Tomorrow you can start looking for it. Every day there will be parents there, in case you have any questions or problems. There won't be any mistakes this time. There will only be E-mail messages full of good news! Each day there will be a new clue about where the treasure is hidden. Follow the clues, and by next week at this time, someone may have found the treasure!"

Molly had the feeling that she wouldn't even need the clues. She had ESP. If she just closed her eyes and concentrated, she would find the treasure. All she had to do was think, think, think!

When Molly got home, she told her parents about Rachel's E-mail from Sonny. They just shook their heads. Then Mrs. Duff said, "Sonny is taking a long time to grow up."

Molly told her parents about the treasure hunt at the fairgrounds. "It's an E-mail game," she said. "All the clues will be on E-mail. One every day."

The Duffs nodded. "We will be there on Saturday and Sunday while you are looking," said her dad.

"I think I'll be the one to find it," said Molly.

"How do you know that?" her dad said, laughing.

"I just feel it," Molly answered.

The next morning before school, Molly turned on the laptop. Sure enough, the first clue was already there!

CHAPTER 10

The Treasure Hunt

"**W**ater's near, and a fence that's white. Look for a building, on your right."

Molly's mind began to spin—water, white fence, a building. Was there a place at the fairgrounds that had all three things?

All day during school, the Pee Wees thought about where to look for the treasure. As soon as school let out, they sped out the door. They went home to get shovels and rakes and warm jackets.

"Be home before dark," called Molly's

dad. "Mr. Peters and Dr. Meyers will be there to answer questions today."

Molly went with Mary Beth and Rachel and Kevin.

Jody's dad took him in the van because of his wheelchair. After his father dropped him off, Jody went right to the carousel. "I found out from doing my report on carousels," he said quietly to Molly, "that sometimes the horses are hollow. The treasure could be inside one of them."

Jody had confided in her! Molly felt good about that, but she didn't think Jody was right about the treasure. Her ESP told her that finding something inside one of the horses would be too hard. He might have to open up every horse!

While Jody searched the carousel, the four friends walked up and down the streets of the fairgrounds.

"There's a white fence around the mid-way," said Kevin.

"There's no water near the midway," said Rachel.

They waved to Dr. Meyers and Mr. Peters. They looked for the white fence and the water.

"The water could be in bottles or something," said Kevin. "It doesn't have to be a river."

"That's good!" said Mary Beth. "Because there *is* no river near here."

Before long, the children got tired and hungry. "This isn't easy," said Molly.

"Tomorrow there will be a new clue," said Kevin. "That will help."

That night, Molly fell into bed, exhausted. The next morning she turned on the laptop. There was another E-mail. In fact, there were two E-mails. One of them had the high-school address at the top.

"Hi," the message said. "Don't you know who I am yet? I saw you looking for the treasure with Kevin and Rachel. But I am going to find it first. From your secret admirer."

Rat's knees, thought Molly! Which Pee Wee was it? She knew it wasn't Kevin or Jody or Tim. That left Roger, Sonny, or Kenny.

Molly would have to worry about it later. Right now she had to read the clue and find that treasure before her admirer did!

"Look for a barn, and rides so dandy. Sometimes even cotton candy."

Rides? Rat's knees, what kind of rides? But *barn*, there was a word she knew! Molly closed her eyes and concentrated.

After school, the Pee Wees met again.

"I have an idea," said Kevin. "I think *rides* means Ferris wheels and stuff, so it must be in the midway, where the merry-go-round is."

"And cotton candy!" said Rachel. "They sell that in the midway too."

"But where is there a barn?" asked Kevin. "The animal barns aren't near the rides."

All of a sudden, Molly knew! And it wasn't her ESP that told her. It was the computer information she had gathered for her report. She was probably the only one who knew that the snack bar in the midway had once been a farmer's barn. That was where they sold cotton candy. And there was a water fountain there, and a white fence outside!

The Pee Wees all sped off in the direction of the Ferris wheel. But Molly knew where she was going. Straight to that snack bar!

The fair had been closed since the summer, but most of the rides and buildings were still there. Molly saw Jody examining the horses on the merry-go-round. She wondered if she should ask him to come with her. Should she share her idea with him? He looked very busy. She decided not to disturb him.

When she got to the snack bar, a few other Pee Wees were digging in the leaves nearby.

"How big is this treasure?" asked Lisa. No one knew.

"Probably the size of a treasure chest," said Tracy.

"Only pirates have treasure chests," scoffed Sonny. "There are no pirates around here."

Molly's grandma always said, "Measure twice, cut once." Molly had to be sure her clues were right. But it was all here, she thought. The barn that no one else knew was a barn, the cotton candy, the water, and the white fence.

The door to the snack bar creaked as Molly pushed it open. Out of the corner of her eye, she saw Mr. Peters watching her from behind. Would he stop her and tell her the snack bar was off-limits? He started walking in the other direction.

It was dark inside. It took a minute for Molly's eyes to adjust to the darkness. When they did, she saw something shine! She bent over and picked up a box from the floor. The box looked like a treasure chest, even though Molly knew there were no pirates around.

She gave a tug at the handle and the chest popped open. Inside, something even shinier sparkled at her! It was a big, glittery coin that looked like gold. And on the front of it were the words PEE WEE TREA-SURE HUNT. CONGRATULATIONS!

Molly screamed, "I found it!" She ran outside, right into the arms of Dr. Meyers!

"Yes, you did!" he said. "We watched you because we thought you were on to something!"

The other Pee Wees came running.

"How did you know it was here?" asked Jody, who reached her first because the carousel was close by.

"My report on barns," she said. "I knew this snack bar was once a farmer's barn."

"Well, congratulations, Molly," said Mr. Peters. "You really followed the clues! There's something else in the chest," he added.

Sure enough, there was an envelope at the bottom of the chest. Molly took it out and opened it. Inside was a piece of paper that said, "Gift certificate for any Halloween costume at Sanders' Department Store."

"Wow!" said Roger. "That means you can get the most expensive one. Like that Batman suit with the wings that really fly."

"How come you didn't tell me you knew where the treasure was?" grumbled Mary Beth. "We're best friends, you know. You should have shared your ESP with me."

"It wasn't ESP after all," said Molly. "It just came to me when I read the clue that said 'Barn.' I remembered some of the stuff I found on the computer. I put two and two together and there it was, in the old barn!"

"Hey, I didn't know this building used to be a barn!" said Tim.

"I didn't find out important stuff like that when I did my report," said Kenny.

"I thought barns were really boring,"

laughed Molly. "Until now! I'm really glad I got that subject for my report."

Mr. Peters dusted off the chest and carried it to the van for Molly. Everyone was patting her on the back and congratulating her. They were all asking her questions at once.

"It didn't take many clues before it was found," said their leader. "I still had about three days' worth of clues to go!"

"Darn," said Sonny, kicking a rock. "I wanted to find that treasure."

"We can't all be winners," said Mr. Peters. "As Scouts, we have to learn to be happy for others."

"Pooh," said Sonny, sticking out his tongue in Molly's direction. "See if I'm ever your secret admirer again!" Then Sonny covered his mouth quickly. "Oops!"

"So you're the letter writer!" said Molly.

"No I'm not," Sonny lied.

"You are too!" said Molly. "I have proof. Mary Beth heard you say it too!" Mary Beth nodded. Sonny ran off and hid.

"Sonny is not your model Pee Wee Scout," said Mary Beth in disgust. "Didn't I tell you it was Sonny who sent those E-mails?"

"But why? He doesn't even like me!" said Molly.

"Maybe he does," said Mary Beth. "My grandma told me that boys always tease the girls they like the best. Love and hate are cousins."

Rat's knees, could this be true? Out of all the Pee Wees, why did Sonny have to be the one to like her? Sticking out his tongue was a funny way of showing it! Well, at least not many of the Pee Wees knew about the things he had said to her. And Molly didn't need ESP to know she had seen the last of the E-mail letters from her secret admirer!

"Next Tuesday is going to be a big day," called Mrs. Peters as the Pee Wees got out of the van. "It is badge day!"

Rat's knees, thought Molly. Pee Wee Scouts was more fun every day! This had been a great week! She had realized she didn't need ESP in order for good things to happen.

She had learned a lot about computers.

She had found the treasure.

She'd have one of the best Halloween costumes in town.

And she would soon have a brand new badge to add to her collection.

There was no doubt about it. She was one lucky girl!

Pee Wee Scout Song

(to the tune of "Old MacDonald Had a Farm")

Scouts are helpers, Scouts have fun
Pee Wee, Pee Wee Scouts!
We sing and play when work is done,
Pee Wee, Pee Wee Scouts!

With a good deed here,
And an errand there,
Here a hand, there a hand,
Everywhere a good hand.

Scouts are helpers, Scouts have fun,
Pee Wee, Pee Wee Scouts!

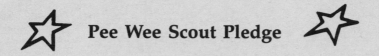# Pee Wee Scout Pledge

We love our country
And our home,
Our school and neighbors too.

As Pee Wee Scouts
We pledge our best
In everything we do.